Hush, Little Alien

Alien

Daniel Kirk

SCHOLASTIC INC.

New York   Toronto   London   Auckland   Sydney   Mexico City   New Delhi   Hong Kong

Hush, little alien,
don't say a word,

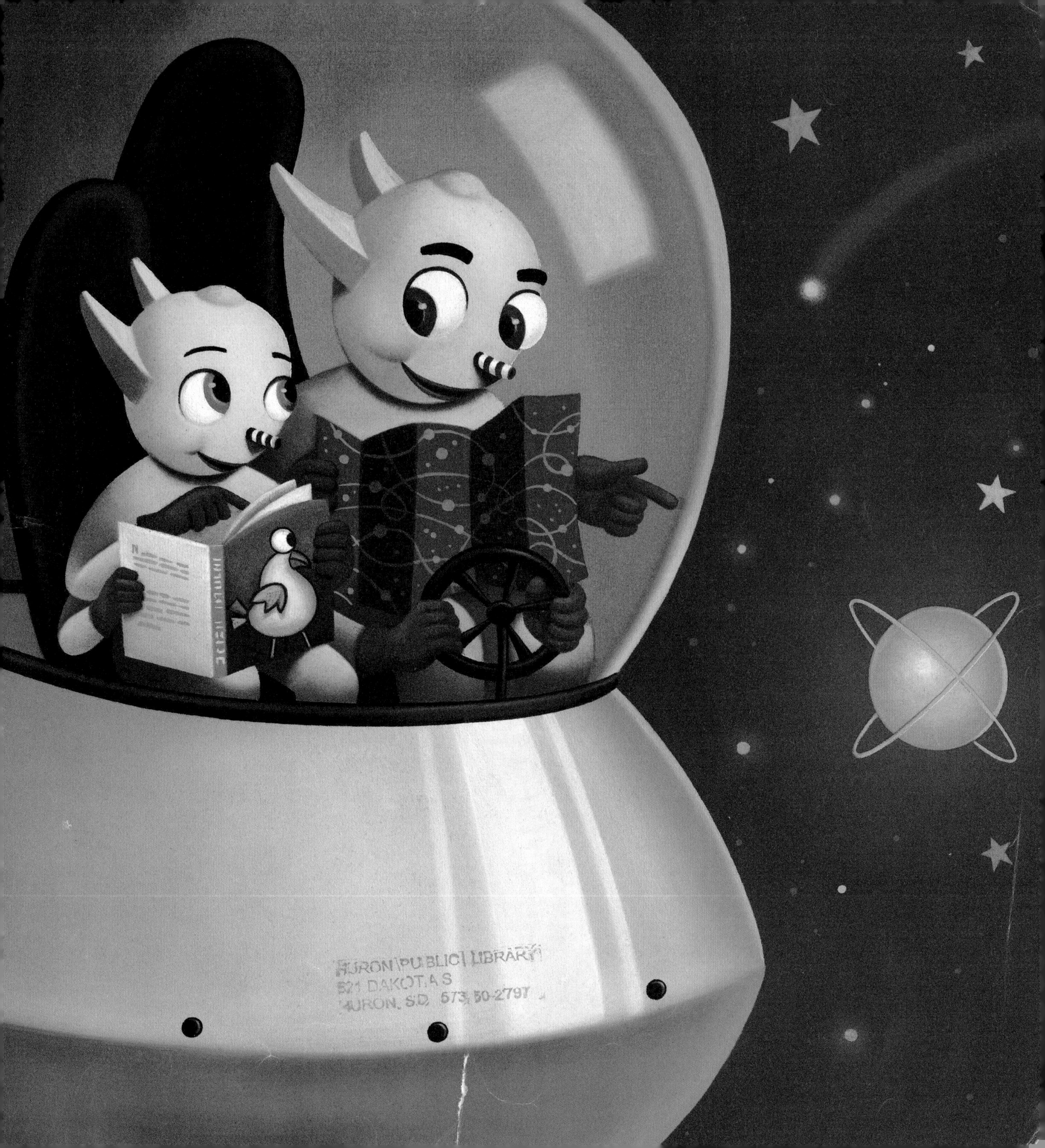

Papa's gonna catch you a goonie bird.

If that goonie bird flies too far,

If that shooting star's too hot,

Papa's gonna

find you an

astronaut!

If that astronaut
should fight,
Papa's gonna bring
you a satellite!

If that
satellite
gets away,
Papa's gonna
take you to
the Milky Way!

With that
tool belt
on your hip,
you're gonna
build a
rocket ship.

And
when
that
rocket
ship
takes
flight,

Papa's gonna give you
a kiss good night!

For Raleigh, the boy with his head in the stars

ISBN 0-439-17676-X

Copyright © 1999 by Daniel Kirk. All rights reserved. Published by Scholastic Inc., 555 Broadway, New York, NY 10012, by arrangement with Hyperion Books for Children, an imprint of Buena Vista Books, Inc. SCHOLASTIC and associated logos are trademarks and/or registered trademarks of Scholastic Inc.

12 11 10 9 8 7 6 5 4 3 2 1   0 1 2 3 4 5/0

Printed in the U.S.A.   09

First Scholastic printing, October 2000

The illustrations in this book were created using oil paint on gessoed Strathmore paper.
This book was set in Triplex 45pt.